Starlight and Candles

The Joys of the Sabbath

by Fran Manushkin   *illustrated by* Jacqueline Chwast

Simon & Schuster Books for Young Readers

My special thanks to Eileen Shmidman, Alan Benjamin,
George Rohr, and Shirley Jacobson for their help.

Simon & Schuster Books for Young Readers
An imprint of Simon & Schuster Children's Publishing Division 1230 Avenue of the Americas New York, NY 10020
Text copyright © 1995 by Fran Manushkin Illustrations copyright © 1995 by Jacqueline Chwast All rights reserved
including the right of reproduction in whole or in part in any form Simon & Schuster Books for Young Readers is a
trademark of Simon & Schuster Designed by Lucille Chomowicz The text of this book is set in Breughel 55 The
illustrations were done in cut paper and watercolor Manufactured in the United States of America
10 9 8 7 6 5 4 3 2 1
Library of Congress Cataloging-in-Publication Data
Manushkin, Fran Starlight and candles : the joys of the Sabbath / by Fran Manushkin ; illustrated by Jacqueline
Chwast p. cm. Summary: Jake and Rosy help to celebrate the Sabbath, their favorite time of the week.
ISBN: 0-689-80274-9 [1. Sabbath—Fiction. 2. Jews—Fiction.] I. Chwast, Jacqueline, ill. II. Title.
PZ7.M3195St 1995 [E]—dc20 94-20232 CIP AC

For my father, Meyer Manushkin –F.M.

In memory of my mother,
Lillian, and my father, William Weiner –J.C.

Jake and Rosy Jacobson always know when the Sabbath is near. The whole house is turned upside down! There is so much to do. At dinner on Thursday, Mama reminds Papa, "Don't forget to bring home the pickles for Grandpa. You know how much he loves his pickles!"

"I won't forget," Papa promises. Then he reminds Jake, "Remember to pick up your good shoes at the shoemaker."

"Right!" Jake nods. "I won't forget."

Then Papa rolls up his sleeves and asks, "Who wants to help me bake *challah*?"

"Me! Me!" Rosy and Jake shout together.

They knead the dough and pound it and then they curl it into braids.

"How many poppy seeds shall we sprinkle on?" Papa asks.

"As many as there are stars!" Rosy answers.

"Rosy, I think you're a poet." Papa smiles.

Later, when the golden loaves come out of the oven, everyone goes to bed. Rosy and Jake drift off to sleep with the scent of challah in the air, a sweet hint of the Sabbath to come.

But on Friday morning, it's still hurry, hurry, hurry! At breakfast, Mama reminds Papa, "Don't forget to pick up the wine!"

"Do I ever forget?" he always answers. Then Papa rushes off to his office, and the children and Mama hurry off to school.

Since Mama is a teacher, she and Rosy and Jake come home at the same time. They finish the Sabbath preparations together and as they do they talk.

"Children," Mama asks, "can you tell me who kept the very first *Shabbat*?"

Rosy ponders the question as she polishes the candlesticks. "Queen Esther?" she answers.

"No! Moses!" yells Jake.

Mama shakes her head as she gives the soup a stir. "Remember how hard God worked creating the sun and the whales and the roses—"

"And the dinosaurs!" adds Jake.

"Of course! The dinosaurs." Mama nods. "Well, on the
seventh day, God blessed the day and rested.

So you see, it is God who kept the first Sabbath."

"And that's why *we* rest, too," comments Jake.

"After you help me set the table," Mama reminds him.

Together they unfold a snowy white tablecloth and place upon it their prettiest china. "Jake, put out some extra chairs," Mama says. "You never know who Papa's bringing home!"

Before Rosy takes her shower, she gives their cat, Shaina, a brushing, because God wants the animals to have a happy Sabbath, too.

Soon it is nearly sunset, the time when the Sabbath begins. This is a good time to remember the children who have no homes to go to when nighttime comes. Jake and Rosy put money for them into the *pushke*.

"Come," Mama says. "It's time to light the candles." Placing a lacy scarf on her head, Mama says, "Candles remind us that God said, 'Let there be light!'"

"And they make the house pretty," adds Rosy.

Three times Mama waves her arms around the candles, gathering in God's great warmth.

With her eyes closed, Mama silently says the blessing. This is always a peaceful moment, and a little mysterious, too.

"*Shabbat Shalom!*" Mama smiles when she opens her eyes. And with kisses for Rosy and Jake, the Sabbath officially begins.

Soon Papa's home, bringing Grandma and Grandpa and some guests. *"Gut Shabbos!"* Grandpa greets everyone in Yiddish, really loud. And he always brings Mama flowers. Grandma comes with hugs and a honey cake.

Gently, Mama and Papa put their hands on the children's heads to give them their Sabbath blessings. They say, "May God bless you and keep you. May God watch over you in kindness."

Jake and Rosy love being blessed, especially if the family has had any fights that week. Mama and Papa's blessings seem to erase all the bad feelings.

Then Grandpa leads the blessing over the wine.
And now comes Rosy's favorite moment: she leads
the singing of *"Lekhah Dodi"*—"Come My Beloved"—
the song that welcomes the Sabbath Bride. Everyone
faces the door, inviting her to enter. It was rabbis long
ago who first greeted the Sabbath Day as though it
were a bride.

Jake leads the singing of *"Shalom Aleichem"*—"Peace Be With You"
—the song that welcomes the Sabbath angels of peace. Jake
imagines them hovering right over his head.

By now everyone is good and hungry! So Rosy and Papa bless the challah and everyone eats a big chunk. Then, as the chicken soup is poured into plates, it's time to hear about everyone's week. And there are always stories, too.

Mama asks Grandma, "Can you tell the children what Shabbat was like when you were a girl?"

Grandma smiles her crinkly smile. "Back in Rumania, I used to watch my grandma make noodles. When they were done, she hung them on the backs of chairs to dry."

"Really!" Rosy is amazed.

"It's true," Grandma insists. "There was no other place to put them. We were so poor back then!"

"Children," Grandpa announces, "I've brought you a surprise." He shows Jake and Rosy a fascinating blue bottle. "When I was a boy, this is how we poured seltzer. Jake, hold out your glass."

Grandpa presses the silver nozzle and seltzer squirts out with a *hisssss*!

"Neat!" Jake laughs.

"Let me try!" begs Rosy.

"Go right ahead," Grandpa agrees. "Just don't spritz my chicken!"

For dessert, there is sweet honey cake and tea, and always more stories.

When the candles flicker out and the stars begin twinkling, everyone gets ready for bed. On Friday nights, Jake and Rosy feel especially cozy and peaceful, sleeping under the blessings of the Sabbath angels.

Saturday morning is peaceful, too. Everyone strolls to synagogue. And there, surrounded by friends, Rosy and Jake pray, "Hear O Israel: the Lord our God, the Lord is One!"

Today Papa is carrying the *Torah*, the word of God. Rosy points out the *yad*, the long silver hand Papa uses to point to the words he reads. "I'm going to hold that at my *Bat Mitzvah*," Rosy tells Grandpa.

Then a bride and groom go up to the *bimah* for a blessing.

"Watch this!" Rosy tells Grandma. "We're going to throw candy to wish the couple a sweet life."

"In *my* day," says Grandma sternly, "we didn't throw candy in *shul*!"

"Times change," Mama reminds her, smiling.

Then the service ends and everyone says, "Shabbat Shalom!" There are so many hugs, the shul feels like one big Jewish family!

"Come over to my house for lunch," Grandma says.

After lunch, the family has all the time in the world together. Papa's briefcase stays shut and Rosy and Jake do no homework.

Instead, everyone takes a Sabbath walk. "On Shabbat," Papa explains, "God doesn't want us to change the world—only to admire it!"

"I admire those ducks a lot." Jake points. "I wish *I* could eat upside down!"

As Papa watches, his face grows wistful. "When I was a boy, my father worked so hard all week fixing furniture. But he never worked on Saturday. 'On the Sabbath,' my papa always told me, 'every man is a king!' I can still remember his strong hand holding mine as we walked home from shul. That was the only time all week that I had my papa to myself."

"And I have *you* on Shabbat!" says Jake softly.

Back home again, Jake and Papa take
a snooze in the big leather chair. Who
wakes up first? Jake! He and Rosy and
their friends still have hours to play
before the day is over.

Later Mama asks, "Has anyone seen three stars in the sky?"

"I see three!" Rosy and Jake both shout. Three stars means it's time to say good-bye to the Sabbath Bride.

Papa lights a special candle and pours wine into a glass. It's sad to say good-bye, so Mama passes around fragrant spices to cheer everyone up.

And when Papa puts the candle out, Shabbat is over.

But next week, there will be another.

And the next. And the next.

Rosy and Jake are sure of that! Why? Because the Sabbath is a sign of the covenant between God and the Jewish people—forever, and ever and ever.

THREE BLESSINGS

THE BLESSING OVER THE CANDLES
Blessed are You, Lord our God, Ruler of the universe, Who has sanctified us by Your commandments and commanded us to kindle the Sabbath lights.

THE BLESSING OVER THE WINE
Blessed are You, Lord our God, Ruler of the Universe, Who creates the fruit of the vine.

THE BLESSING OVER THE BREAD
Blessed are You, Lord our God, Ruler of the Universe, Who brings forth bread from the earth.

GLOSSARY

Bat Mitzvah—The Hebrew words for "daughter of the covenant." The Bat Mitzvah ceremony is held when a girl reaches the age of twelve-and-a-half or thirteen.

bimah—The raised platform in the synagogue where the Torah is read.

challah—An egg bread that is eaten on Shabbat and other Jewish festivals.

Gut Shabbos—A good Sabbath to you, in Yiddish.

pushke—A container where money is put for the poor.

Shabbat—The Sabbath

Shabbat Shalom—A warm greeting that means, A peaceful Sabbath to you.

shul—Yiddish for synagogue

Torah—Teachings; the scroll on which the word of God is written.

yad—The silver hand the Torah reader uses to point to the words on the scroll.